Clarion Books • An Imprint of HarperCollins Publishers • Boston New York

Maybe Something BEAUTIFUL

HOW ART TRANSFORMED A NEIGHBORHOOD

BY F. Isabel Campoy
AND Theresa Howell

ILLUSTRATED BY
Rafael López

In the heart of a gray city, there lived a girl
who loved to doodle, draw, color, and paint.
Every time she saw a blank piece of paper,
Mira thought to herself,
Hmm, maybe . . .
And because of this, her room was filled with color
and her heart was filled with joy.

On her way to school one day,
Mira gave a round apple to Mr. Henry,
the owner of the shop down the street.
She gave a flower to Ms. López,
the lady with the sparkling eyes.

She gave a songbird to Mr. Sax
and a red heart to the policeman
who walked up and down the streets.

On her way home, Mira taped a glowing sun
onto the wall hiding in the shadows.

Her city was less gray—but not much.

The next day, Mira saw a man
with a pocket full of paintbrushes.
He gazed at the wall.
He looked at her sun.
He held his fingers up in a square
and peered through them.
"Hmm . . ." he said thoughtfully.
"What do you see?" Mira asked.
"Maybe . . . something beautiful,"
the man replied.

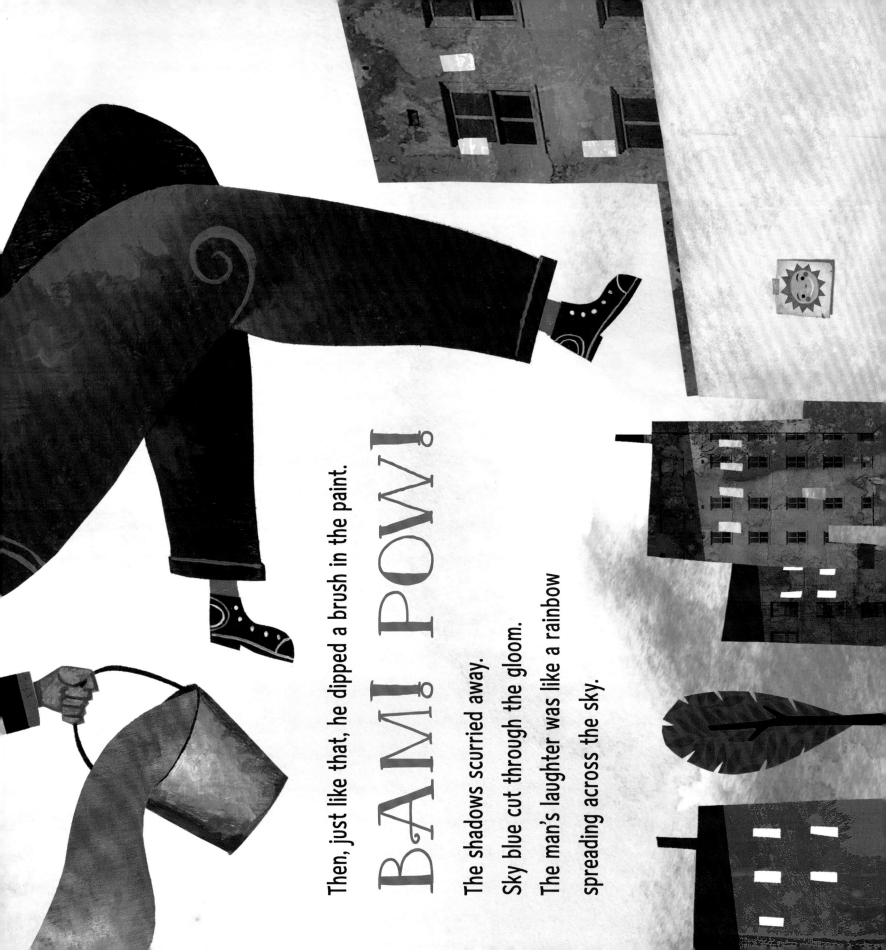

Then, just like that, he dipped a brush in the paint.

BAM! POW!

The shadows scurried away.
Sky blue cut through the gloom.
The man's laughter was like a rainbow
spreading across the sky.

"Who are you?" Mira asked.

"I'm an artist," he said. "A muralist.
I paint on walls!"

"I'm an artist too," she told him.

He handed Mira a brush.

"THEN COME ON!"

Mira dipped it in the loudest color she saw.

YOW-WEE!

The wall lit up like sunshine.

As the man drew pictures on the bricks,
Mira added color, punch, and pizzazz!
Soon Mr. Sax joined in.
Then came others.
Everyone painted to the rhythm.
Salsa, merengue, bebop!

Even Mira's mama painted
and danced the cha-cha-cha!
The whole neighborhood
became a giant block party.

Until . . .

. . . the policeman walked up.

"Excuse me," he said.
The music stopped. Mira put her brush down.
They were surely in trouble.
The officer cleared his throat, then paused.

"May I paint with you?" he asked.
So Mira handed him a paintbrush.
And the music started again.

Teachers and papas jumped in.

Babies too!

Mira and the man handed out brush after brush.

Color spread throughout the streets.

So did joy.

Wherever Mira and the man went,

art followed like the string of a kite.

After they colored the walls,

they painted utility boxes and benches.

They decorated sidewalks with poetry and shine.

And everyone danced.

Together, they created something more beautiful than they had ever imagined.

When their clothes were splattered with a million colors,
everyone sat down to rest—except the muralist.
His eyes sparkled.
"You, my friends, are all artists," he told them.
"The world is your canvas."
He smiled wide, then pulled everything together
in big, sweeping motions.
His paintbrush was like a magic wand.

When he was finished, Mira added
one more bird, way up in the sky.
Maybe, she thought. *Just maybe . . .*

A NOTE FROM THE AUTHORS

Maybe Something Beautiful is based on a true story. At one time, the colorful East Village near downtown San Diego, California, did not have murals on the walls, nor quotes from Gandhi, Martin Luther King, and César Chávez written on the sidewalks. Benches were not the works of art you can see now, and people living in the area were not part of the vibrant community that they are today. Instead, the streets were gray and drab. But one day, a husband-wife-team—he an artist, she a graphic designer and community leader—moved in and transformed their neighborhood into a place of beauty.

Rafael and Candice López designed a plan to bring people together to create art so that their neighborhood could become a better place for all to live. They held meetings in their home to share their idea. Everyone was invited—police officers, graffiti artists, teachers, single parents, children, homeless people, and more. With the help of many, the Urban Art Trail was born, and volunteers of all ages, races, and walks of life committed themselves to a common goal: reviving their community through art.

First came murals entitled *The Joy of Urban Living* and *The Strength of the Women*. Then the community painted

utility boxes and benches bright colors. They crafted mosaics around the trees along the streets. Rafael and Candice had noticed that in their neighborhood, people often looked down at the ground as they walked, so they painted poems in calligraphy on the sidewalks. Little by little, the entire neighborhood became a work of art—and an inspiration to those who lived there.

The impact of art in the neighborhood grew. Some of the painted benches were auctioned off, and the money provided classes and scholarships for at-risk students who had an interest in art. Visitors came to admire; donations

big and small came in. And what had once seemed to be an impossible dream became a trademark of San Diego's East Village.

The movement prompted by the Urban Art Trail spread far and wide. Communities throughout the United States have commissioned Rafael's murals, and neighborhoods as far away as Canada and Australia have implemented the model of community-based art.

Maybe Something Beautiful, illustrated by the muralist who inspired it, was written in honor of Rafael and Candice López and all the quiet leaders in our neighborhoods. It is an invitation to transform not only the walls and streets of our cities but also the minds and hearts of communities.

For Alma Flor Ada, partner in magical transformations —F.I.C.

For Ella and Sylvia, who bring art and light into my life every day —T.H.

For the playground of possibility —R.L.

Design by Sharismar Rodriguez • Library of Congress Cataloging-in-Publication Data: Campoy, F. Isabel, author. Maybe something beautiful / by F. Isabel Campoy and Theresa Howell ; illustrated by Rafael López. pages cm Summary: "Mira lives in a gray and hopeless urban community until a muralist arrives and, along with his paints and brushes, brings color, joy, and togetherness to Mira and her neighbors."— Provided by publisher ISBN 978-0-544-35769-3 [1. Neighborhoods—Fiction. 2. City and town life—Fiction. 3. Mural painting and decoration—Fiction.] I. Howell, Theresa, 1974- author. II. López, Rafael, 1961- illustrator. III. Title. PZ7.C16153May 2016 [E]—dc23 2015000958 • Manufactured in Italy • 21 •